Homes

discovered through
Science

Karen Bryant-Mole

Contents

A & C Black • London

Homes

Homes are places where people live. We often use our homes and the things in them without even thinking about how or why they work.

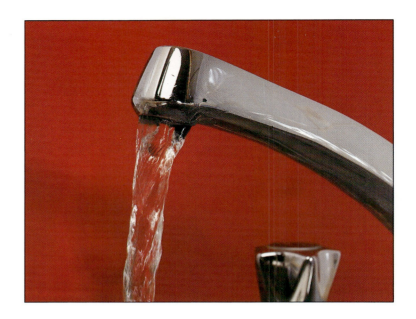

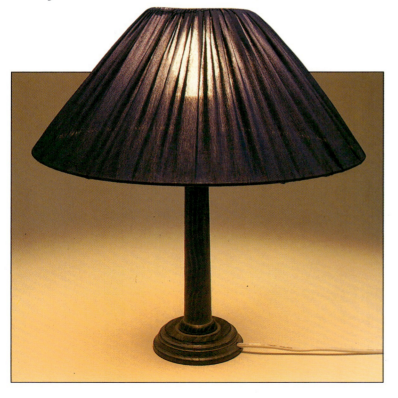

You turn on a tap and water comes out.
Where does it come from?

You press a switch and a bulb lights up.
How does this happen?

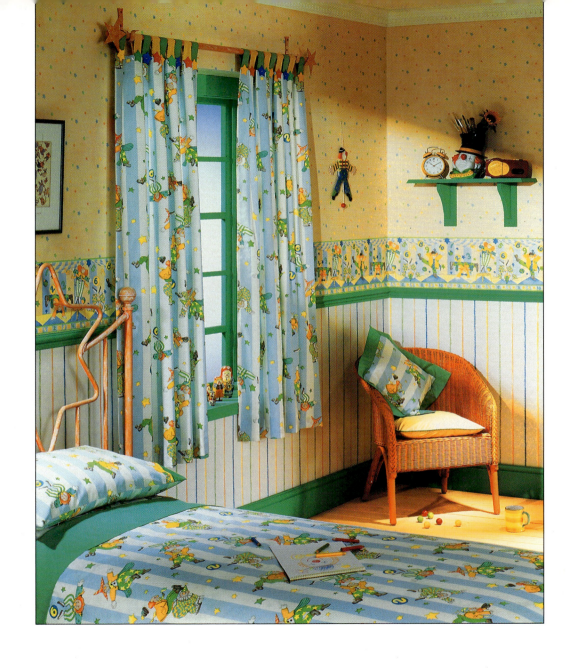

The sheets on your bed are made from fabric.
Why is fabric a good material for sheets?

This book will answer these and other questions as it explores the science that can be found in your home.

Electricity

Almost all homes have electricity.
Electricity has many different uses.

Power lines

Electricity is made in buildings called power stations.
The electricity travels to our homes along special wires, known as power lines.
Power lines can be buried underground or carried over the ground on tall pylons.

Dangerous

Electricity is very useful but it can also be very dangerous.
Electricity can give a person an electric shock.
Electric shocks can kill.

Homes

Many of the things in our homes need electricity to make them work.
Have a look around your home.
How many things would stop working if there was no electricity?

Never play with plugs, lights or electrical equipment.

Lighting

We need light to help us see around our homes.

Sunlight
During the day, sunlight helps us to see. Sunlight comes into our homes through the windows.

Lights

At night, or when there is not much sunlight, we use electric light bulbs. Electricity passes through a thin wire in the light bulb. This makes the wire heat up and give off light.

Luminous

Objects that give out their own light are called luminous objects. Lamps and candles are luminous.

Computer screens and televisions are luminous, too.

Water

We all use water every day of our lives.

Pipes
Water is stored in large lakes, called reservoirs.
It is cleaned and sent along underground pipes to our homes.
When we turn on the tap, water flows out.

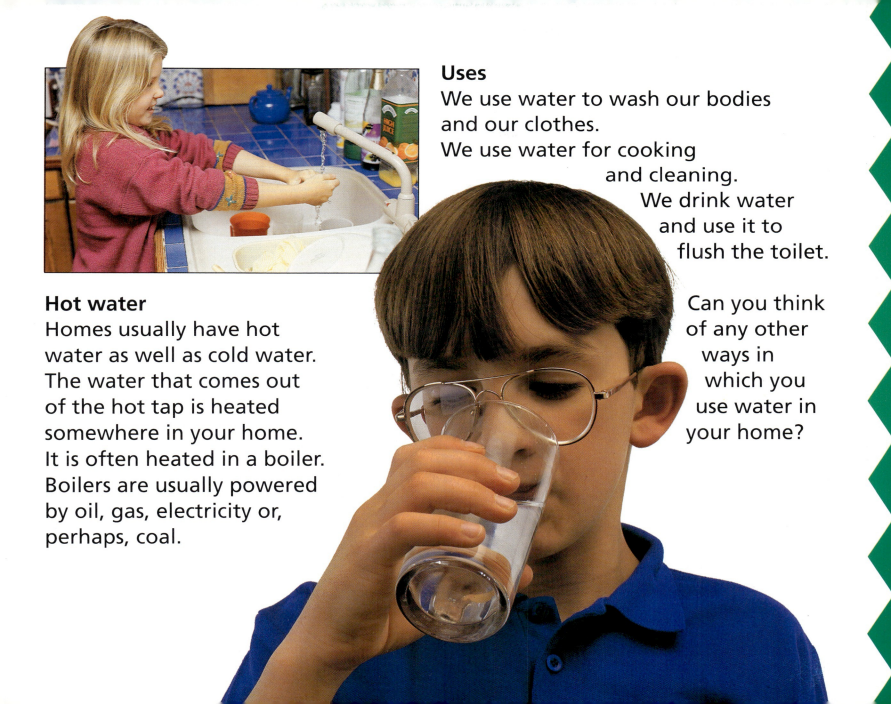

Uses

We use water to wash our bodies and our clothes.
We use water for cooking and cleaning.
We drink water and use it to flush the toilet.

Hot water

Homes usually have hot water as well as cold water. The water that comes out of the hot tap is heated somewhere in your home. It is often heated in a boiler. Boilers are usually powered by oil, gas, electricity or, perhaps, coal.

Can you think of any other ways in which you use water in your home?

Keeping warm

When the weather is cold, we need to heat our homes.

Heating
Some people use fires to heat their homes.

In the past, all homes were heated by coal fires. Today, lots of people have gas fires or electric fires.

Some electric heaters, like the one in this picture, push warm air into the room.

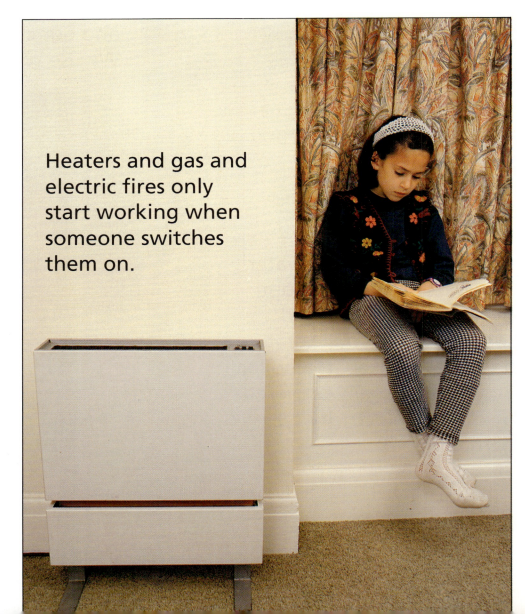

Heaters and gas and electric fires only start working when someone switches them on.

Central heating

Many people have central heating.
Central heating usually uses hot water from the boiler to warm up radiators in all the rooms.
People can set a timer that switches the central heating on and off for them.

Hot water bottles

There are other ways to keep warm at home.
Beds can be warmed by an electric blanket or by a hot water bottle.
We can keep our bodies warm by wearing lots of layers of clothes.

Cooking

People use different sorts of cookers to cook their food. There are gas cookers, electric cookers, microwave ovens and even barbecues.

Heating

All food that is cooked has to be heated. There are many ways to heat food. For instance, food can be boiled, baked, steamed, fried or microwaved.

Cooked food

Once food has been cooked, it cannot be uncooked.
This boiled egg will still be cooked, even when it has cooled down.

Changes

Cooking makes changes happen to food. Sometimes these changes make the food look very different.

This runny cake mixture will turn into a solid cake when it is heated in the oven.

Machines

We use lots of machines
around our homes.
Many of these machines use
energy from electricity
to turn a motor.

Cleaning
This vacuum cleaner has
a motor.
The motor turns a fan
which sucks air into the
vacuum cleaner.
As the air is sucked in, dust
and dirt are sucked in, too.

**Never switch on a machine in
your home unless a grown-up
is with you.
Machines can be very
dangerous.**

Washing clothes

Washing machines have motors
that spin a metal drum.
The drum turns quite slowly
to move the washing about
in the water.
It then turns quickly to spin
the water out of the clothes.

Cooking

A motor inside this food processor
turns the mixing blades.
Other pieces of cooking equipment
that have small motors include
coffee grinders, electric whisks and
electric carving knives.

Pushes and pulls

Every day, around
our homes,
we push things and
pull things.
In science, pushes
and pulls are known
as forces.

Open and close
We use pushes and
pulls to open and
close doors.
We pull on handles
or knobs to open
a drawer and push
to close it.

On and off

Many things are turned on or off by pushing buttons or switches. This light switch has to be pressed. Pressing is a type of pushing.

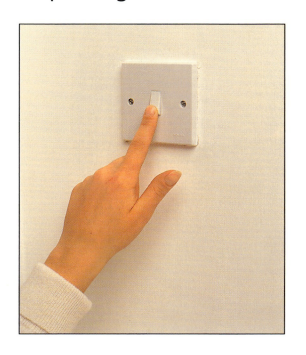

Turning

Forces are also needed to make something turn. When you turn on a tap, you pull and push with your fingers and thumbs.

What other things do you do around the home that need pushes and pulls?

Sound

Lots of different types of sound can be heard in our homes.

Objects

Many of the sounds in our homes are made by objects.

This clock makes a ticking sound.
Door bells ring.
Tape recorders play music.
Machines whirr.

Living things

Sounds are made by the people who live in our home.

They talk, laugh, cry and shout.
Other living creatures, such as cats and dogs, make sounds, too.

Loud and soft

Some sounds, like the click of a switch, are soft.
Others, such as the ring of a telephone, are loud.
But, if you move away from a ringing telephone, it starts to sound quieter.
The further you are from whatever is making the sound, the quieter it seems.

Materials

Our homes and the things in them are made from materials.
Different materials have different names.

Wood
These kitchen cupboards are made from wood.

Wood is used to make many types of furniture. It is also used to make floors, doors and other parts of our homes.

Metal
All of these things have been made from metal.
There are many different types of metal.
Most of these things are made from stainless steel.

Clay

Plates, bowls, cups, saucers and vases are often made from clay.

Clay is a special type of earth that can be made into all sorts of different shapes.

It is often given a coating, called a glaze.

Find out the names of other materials that have been used to make things in your home.

Choosing materials

There is usually a good reason why something is made from a particular material.

Glass
Windows are usually made from glass. Glass is see-through. It is waterproof, too, so it doesn't let in the rain.

Plastic
Plastic can be made into lots of different shapes.
It doesn't usually break, so it is a good material for young children's toys.

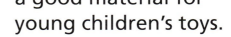

Fabric

Fabric is used to make curtains, tablecloths, sheets and duvets.

Fabric is soft and can be cut and sewn into many different shapes.

Most fabric is easy to wash.

A lot of work, thought and science has gone into making our homes the comfortable places they are today.

Glossary

blade a thin, flat part of a machine, often used for cutting

clay a special type of earth

coffee grinder a machine that turns coffee beans into powder

drum the part of a washing machine that the clothes go into

fabric cloth

glaze a shiny, waterproof layer often found on objects made from clay

power station a building where electricity is made

Index

How to use this book

Each book in this series takes a familiar topic or theme and focuses on one area of the curriculum: science, art and technology, geography or history. The books are intended as starting points, illustrating some of the many different angles from which a topic can be studied. They should act as springboards for further investigation, activity or information seeking.

The following list of books may prove useful.

Further books to read

Series	Title	Author	Publisher
Find Out About	all titles	Henry Pluckrose	Watts
Jump! Science	Experiment with Electricity	B. Murphy	Watts
Science Activities	Science in the Kitchen	R. Heddle	Usborne
Science All Around Me	all titles	K. Bryant-Mole	Heinemann
Starting Point Science	Where Does Electricity Come From?	S. Mayes	Usborne
Starting Science	Electricity and Magnetism Hot and Cold Light Materials	Davies & Oldfield	Wayland
Talkabout	Light	H. Pluckrose	Watts
Threads	Bricks Clay Glass Plastics Wood	T. Cash A. Dixon J. Chandler T. Cash T. Jennings	A&C Black
Toppers	Homes	N. Baxter	Watts